A Snow Story

By Melvin J. Leavitt

Illustrated by Jo Ellen McAllister Stammen

Simon & Schuster Books for Young Readers

SIMON & SCHUSTER BOOKS FOR YOUNG READERS

An imprint of Simon & Schuster Children's Publishing Division

1230 Avenue of the Americas, New York, NY 10020

Designed by Christy Hale

The text of this book is set in 18-point Lapidary.

The illustrations are rendered in colored pencil.

Manufactured in the United States of America.

10 9 8 7 6 5 4 3 2 1

Library of Congress Cataloging-in-Publication Data

Leavitt, Melvin.

A snow story / Melvin J. Leavitt ; illustrated by Jo Ellen
McAllister Stammen.

p.   cm.

Summary: A young boy begins writing poems in the snow that are
read and responded to by wildlife, and he continues writing them
throughout his life.

ISBN 0-689-80296-X

[1. Snow—Fiction.   2. Poetry—Fiction.]   I. Stammen, Jo Ellen
McAllister, ill.   II. Title.

PZ7.L4657Sn   1995

[E]—dc20   94-21532

                                                         CIP

                                                         AC

JOHNNY was a quiet boy. Polite. Thoughtful. He worked hard on his father's farm each day, and in the evenings he read. He smiled easily, but didn't laugh much. Often his gray eyes would get a faraway look in them, and his mother would say, "Dreams are for sleep time, boy."

Sometimes in January or February on the day after a big storm, when the drifts lay as clean and white as the streets of heaven, Johnny would beat a path onto the frozen lake and walk back and forth.

"What were you doing out there?" his mother would ask.

"I was writing a poem," he would answer.

"A poem?"

"In the snow. With my boots."

Then his mother would frown and say, "If you don't want to tell me, son, just say so. Don't make up smart-aleck answers." But she was a busy woman and really not all that curious.

One morning in spring when the last of the ice and snow
had melted and the trees shimmered in a haze of new green,
Johnny and his father began plowing their fields.

"Look to the lake!" his father exclaimed, ankle-deep in rich
black soil. "The ducks have gone mad!"

The wild ducks on the lake
were exploding into the air, flapping
in lopsided spirals and rolling loops,
then diving to dip their wing tips in water
before climbing again. Up and down they went,
sketching dark lines across the sky.

"What ails them?" Johnny's father asked.

Johnny adjusted the harness on the plow horse and squinted into the morning sun. "I don't know," he said cautiously, "but I wrote poems in the lake snow last winter before it melted."

Johnny's father looked at him oddly and turned back to work.

Johnny grew up and married a woman he loved, and they worked hard to build a good life together. They were as close to each other as ever butter was to bread.

But sometimes in January or February on the day after a big storm, when fir trees rose from the drifts like white giants, Johnny would leave his bride behind, walk onto the frozen lake, and stomp around in the snow.

"What were you doing out there, Johnny?" his wife would ask.

"Writing a poem," he would answer.

"A poem?"

"In the snow. With my boots."

"Oh, you're such a tease!" she would giggle, and let it go at that.

One day in early summer, Johnny and his wife lay dozing on the riverbank, cane fishing poles propped on forked sticks. Amber sunlight sifted through a canopy of leaves, dappling the slow water near the shore.

"Look, Johnny!" his wife shouted. "The fish are going crazy!"

High above the river, the sky was full of fish leaping, twisting, shaking, and falling in cascades of silver and rose. Again and again they leaped, their shining bodies flinging rainbow spray.

"What's gotten into them?" Johnny's wife asked.

Johnny rubbed his chin. "I don't know," he said. "But I wrote poems in the lake snow last winter, and the lake water feeds the river."

Johnny's wife laughed and hugged the strange man she had married.

Years passed, and Johnny and his wife raised six children. He loved them all and did his best to feed and clothe them and teach them right from wrong. Together the whole family sowed their fields in the spring, hoed them in the summer, and harvested them in the fall.

But sometimes in January or February on the day after a big storm, when snow fell like cherry blossoms from bare branches, Johnny would leave his family behind, wade through the drifts on the frozen lake, and stride about.

"What were you doing out there, Dad?" his children would ask.

"Writing a poem," he would answer.

"A poem?"

"In the snow. With my boots."

They would shake their heads and smile. "Sure, Dad. Sure you were."

One afternoon in autumn, Johnny and his oldest son loaded their biggest, roundest, ripest pumpkins into the bed of a battered pickup. Off through the golden woods they rattled, down long, leafy roads to a wide bay where the river met the sea. The sun was just touching the waves as they began unloading the pickup at a farmers' market.

"Look!" cried Johnny's son, almost dropping a prize pumpkin. "The otters are going berserk!"

River otters were sliding down slick banks. Up the bay, sea otters came swimming with the tide. They met and mingled in a strange ballet and intertwined in games of tag. Their black wakes drew curlicues across the red-gold water—like words in an unknown language.

"What's wrong with them?" Johnny's son asked.

Johnny hefted a fat orange pumpkin and squinted into the setting sun. "I don't know," he said, "but I wrote poems in the lake snow last winter, and the lake water feeds the river, and the river water feeds the sea."

When Johnny grew too old to farm much anymore, he
would sit reading for hours, and that faraway look was often
in his eyes. His wife and children and grandchildren would
come sit with him when they could, and he was glad to have
their quiet company.

But sometimes in January or February on the day after a big storm, when breath came in ghostly clouds against a blue sky, he would leave everyone behind, hobble slowly through the snow onto the frozen lake, and walk painfully about.

"What were you doing out there, Grandpa?" his grandchildren would ask.

"Writing a poem," he would answer.

"A poem?"

"In the snow. With my boots."

"Grandpa, you're so funny!" his grandchildren would laugh, and then return to their games.

One winter night Johnny died, and he was both mourned and missed. For as winter followed winter, his walks in the snow were remembered with wonder. Sometimes in January or February on the day after a big storm, when the snow lay fiery white and window-deep, someone might look to the lake and say, "If Great-grandpa were alive, he'd be out there stomping around right now."

Then someone else would smile and go to the window. "What do you think he was really doing out there?"

But the poems—all of them—layer
on layer, year on year, had melted
each spring into the lake and run
from the lake into the river and from
the river into the sea. There whales
read them in the deep currents. Seals
frolicked in and out and up and down
the snowy silver of them.

And dolphins, leaping in the sun over light-filled waves,
still recite some of the best lines to this very day.

Date Due